Do You Believe in Unicorns?

Bethanie Deeney Murguia

CANDLEWICK PRESS

For Thunder Paws

First edition 2018

Library of Congress Catalog Card Number pending
ISBN 978-0-7636-9468-5

18 19 20 21 22 23 APS 10 9 8 7 6 5 4 3 2 1

Printed in Humen, Dongguan, China

This book was typeset in Archer Book.
The illustrations were done in pen and ink and watercolor.

Candlewick Press
99 Dover Street
Somerville, Massachusetts 02144

visit us at www.candlewick.com

Hey, look—
it's a horse in a hat.

No, I do *not* think it could be
a unicorn in disguise.
That's ridiculous.

It's just a horse — a horse who
woke up with messy hair.
That's why it's wearing a hat.

Tell me this — why would a unicorn
want to *hide* its horn?

You think unicorns like to
keep people guessing?
I think it's just a horse whose
favorite color is red.

Or a horse who doesn't
want the sun in its eyes.

Do you really think it could be
that easy to find a unicorn?

Let's be realistic. It's probably
a horse trying to keep its head dry.

I do think a horse would take
its hat off for tea, though. . . .

So I suppose I can't be completely, entirely certain it's *not* a unicorn.

Oh, thank goodness.
Now we'll know for sure.

It's a . . .

Hold on a minute.
Maybe you can only see unicorns . . .

if you believe in them.